HarperCollins Children's Books, a division of HarperCollins Publishers, 195 Broadway, New York, NY 10007

HarperCollins Publishers, Macken House, 39/40 Mayor Street Upper, Dublin 1, D01 C9W8, Ireland

Pete the Cat and the Cookie Catastrophe

harpercollins.com

Library of Congress Control Number: 2025951080
ISBN 978-0-06-335058-8

The artist used pen and ink with watercolor and acrylic paint on 300lb
press paper to create the illustrations for this book.

26 27 28 29 30 PC 10 9 8 7 6 5 4 3 2 1
First Edition

Pete the Cat and the Cookie Catastrophe

Kimberly & James Dean

HARPER
An Imprint of HarperCollinsPublishers

It was a groovy sunny day.

Pete had volunteered to bake cookies for the annual Cookie Fest. His Nana's cookie recipe was the best!

But making cookies takes some time.

You mix,

you stir,

you wait!

You roll the dough,

then shape and bake. . . .

There is so much waiting,
for goodness' sake!

Pete did not want to wait!

Pete did not want to bake all day!

Pete wanted to go out and play!

Pete had a groovy, brilliant plan.
"I'll build a cookie machine! I know I can!"

It'll mix, stir, shape, and bake. Less time than Nana's recipe would take!

Push a button, twist a dial. It will bake cookies with groovy style.

Pete tinkered...

...and tinkered...

. . . and tinkered some more.

BEHOLD! The Cookie-O-Matic!

It's cool, it's groovy, it's fantastic!

It stirs! It bakes! It's really fast! Waiting is now a thing of the past!

The Cookie-O-Matic was ready to go!

Pete tossed the sugar

and chips into the dough.

Pete pushed the button, and
the lights started to glow!

The Cookie-O-Matic blinked and buzzed and started to bake.

But then the Cookie-O-Matic started to shake!

KA-BOOM!
ON
OFF

HOT

It started to pop. It made a loud ROAR.

Then cookies shot out the door!

Cookies here, cookies there.
Cookies flying through the air!

"UH-OH!" said Pete. "This isn't good!"

He watched as cookies covered the neighborhood.

Cookies were in the trees and on the school.

Cookies were even in the pool!
This wasn't COOL!

Pete's friends came running to help.

"Hey, Pete, don't stress!" they said.
"We will help clean up this mess!"

Let's bake cookies the simple way. . .

. . . and while we wait, we can play!

Pete and his friends played a game.

They sang some songs and had some fun.

DING! And in a flash, the cookies were done!

The friends ate their cookies. YUM!

And Pete said,

"Take it slow. That's

the groovy way to go!"